Christine Naumann-Villemin began her career as a speech therapist, inventing stories for her young patients. Today, Christine is a professor and librarian living in France. She tests her story ideas on her three children, cat, and hamster.

Kris Di Giacomo is an American who has lived in Paris since childhood. She has illustrated over twenty-five picture books, including *Take Away the A* (Enchanted Lion), which was named an ALA Notable Book in 2015. Kris divides her time between working on new books and meeting her readers at schools and book fairs throughout France. Visit her website at www.krisdigiacomo.com.

For Vero and Chico, my dear friends
C.N.-V.

To good neighbors and to little city rabbits
K.D.G.

First published in the United States in 2017 by Eerdmans Books for Young Readers,
an imprint of Wm. B. Eerdmans Publishing Co.
2140 Oak Industrial Dr. NE, Grand Rapids, Michigan 49505
www.eerdmans.com/youngreaders

Text by Christine Naumann-Villemin
Illustrations by Kris Di Giacomo
Originally published in France in 2011 by Éditions Kaléidoscope
under the title *Quand le Loup a Faim*
© 2011 Kaléidoscope

Manufactured at Tien Wah Press in Malaysia

17 18 19 20 21 22 23   9 8 7 6 5 4 3 2 1

ISBN 978-0-8028-5482-7

A catalog record of this book is available from the Library of Congress.

Display type set in Rough Draught and Dark Roast
Text type set in Century Gothic and Landliebe

When a Wolf is Hungry

Written by **Christine Naumann-Villemin**
Illustrated by **Kris Di Giacomo**

Eerdmans Books for Young Readers
Grand Rapids, Michigan

One Sunday morning, Edmond Bigsnout, lone wolf, left his home in the woods with a great big knife in his paw.

Edmond had a hankering for some rabbit.

Not just any ordinary cottontail, though. What he craved was a grain-fed, silky-haired rabbit, one with just a hint of sweetness. A city bunny.

He hopped on his bike and headed for the city,
determined to find one.

He stopped in front of a tall apartment building.
He checked the names next to the buzzers
and found exactly what he was looking for:

Max Omatose, miniature rabbit
5th floor

Oh, Edmond was so happy!
With the point of his knife,
he pressed the button for the elevator.

Ding!

Inside the elevator, he set down the
knife and adjusted his bow tie.
(Just because a wolf is hungry,
that doesn't mean he can't be
fashionable.)

But of course, he forgot his knife
in the elevator.

Ding!

The turkey from the third floor was on her way home from the bakery. "Oh! A knife! That's just what I need to cut this cake!"

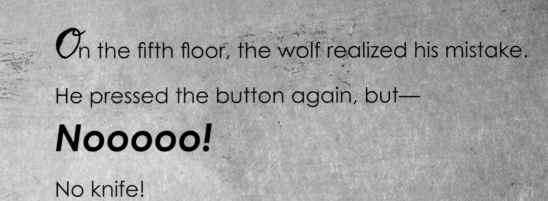

On the fifth floor, the wolf realized his mistake.

He pressed the button again, but—

Nooooo!

No knife!

It doesn't matter, thought Edmond,
I'll pedal home lickety-split and get my chainsaw—
sliced rabbit is delicious too!

In no time at all, Edmond was back.

Ding!

The bear from the fourth floor!

"Good day, sir! Are you our new neighbor?"

"No . . . uh . . . I mean . . . yes . . ." said the wolf, lying through his teeth.

"Welcome to the building! My, that's a nice chainsaw you have there. What did you need it for?"

"To slice a rab . . . uh . . . to trim my . . ."

"Would you mind terribly if I borrowed it until this evening? I have a hedge to trim on the roof."

"Not at all . . ."

Argh.

How annoying!

Edmond got out of the elevator on the ground floor.

Rope! I need a rope! he thought.

To tie up that rabbit.

And eat him in peace.

The wolf pedaled back, but he was getting hungrier and hungrier. All this biking certainly worked up an appetite!

Ding!

*T*here, in the elevator, was a skunk. His hands were quite full.

"Hello, are you the new neighbor?"

"Yes, yes," grumbled Edmond.

"Delighted to meet you. Oh, look, you have some rope! Any chance I could have it? This great big package is such a nuisance."

Drat!

"I suppose so," sighed the wolf.

The skunk was so pleased that he let out a little air.

Edmond decided to take the stairs back down—
the elevator had gotten a bit too . . . smelly.

Oh well, never mind.
The wolf rushed home to get his big pot.
He would just throw the rabbit in and eat him whole.
No more messing around!

$\mathcal{T}$he wolf was all out of breath
by the time he got back.

A large cow was waiting for the elevator.
"Oh! Hello, Mr. . . . ?"

"Edmond Bigsnout."

"A new neighbor! How delightful! And what a lovely pot!"

"It is, isn't it?"

"Tell me, neighbor, would it be too forward of me
to ask to borrow it?"

"Well, I sort of need it . . ."

"What a shame! My husband will be terribly upset.
But no matter—you'll explain it to him yourself,
won't you?"

"Never mind! Just take it!"

Drat, drat, drat. Dang, drat, rats!
All right, it's barbecue time! thought Edmond.
I'm going to grill that rabbit just as he is,
ears and tail and all!

So Edmond went home, tied a trailer to his bike,
and pedaled as fast as he could back to the city.

Ding!

Right there in front of him was Miss Eyestopper, who had a box of matches in her paw.

"Ooh! How fancy! Do you live here? With your parents?"

"Uh . . . no, all by myself . . ." stammered Edmond.

"How interesting . . ." said the lovely young wolf.

"Oh . . . is that a grill? Just what I was looking for. Thank you, Mr. Wolf—you are too kind! I do hope I'll be seeing you around."

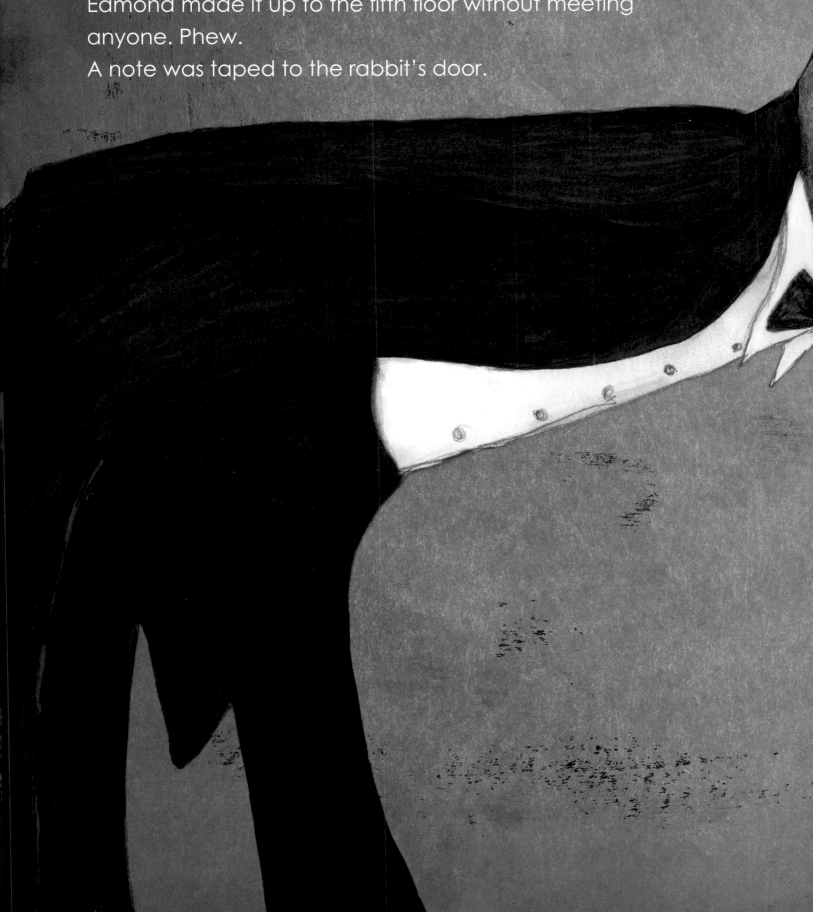

Aargh!

"Enough is enough! I'm going to eat him raw—
with a little mustard, and that's it!"
Edmond made it up to the fifth floor without meeting
anyone. Phew.
A note was taped to the rabbit's door.

"To the roof I go, my little rabbit,
to eat you at last!"

"Our new neighbor! Please join us!"

"Come over here, dear friend!
Oh! You even brought mustard!"

"How neighborly of you!"

"Don't be shy, we won't eat you!"

FOR SALE

~~*Famished*~~

FINISHED.